For Caroline – M.S.

First published 2013 by Macmillan Children's Books
a division of Macmillan Publishers Limited
20 New Wharf Road, London N1 9RR
Basingstoke and Oxford
Associated companies throughout the world
www.panmacmillan.com

ISBN: 978-0-230-75458-4

3 5 7 9 8 6 4 2

A CIP catalogue record for this book is available from the British Library.

Printed in China

Mike Smith

THE HUNDRED DECKER BUS

MACMILLAN
CHILDREN'S
BOOKS

It was a Tuesday morning like any other.

As usual, the bus driver finished his cup of tea at 5.57.

As usual, he put on his jacket at 5.58.

And, as usual, he clambered onto his double-decker bus at 5.59.

At six o'clock exactly, he started the engine
and drove out of the bus station.

Just like every day, the man with the huge red tie got on at the roundabout.

Just like every day, the lady with the pram got on at the library.

And just like every day, the noisy children got on at Clover Drive.

The driver sighed. He was bored with every day being the same. "If only we were in that hot air balloon," he thought, "we could float up and away and anywhere we like."

Then he noticed a little road that he had never seen before. "I wonder where that goes," he thought.

The bus driver turned down the little road. This was not his usual route. It was exciting! Before long, the bus was heading out of the city and into the countryside.

"Excuse me," said the man in the red tie, "where are we going?"
"I don't know," replied the driver cheerfully. "Anywhere!"

The bus carried on. It came to new and different towns with new and different bus stops. This was an adventure!

Before long, the bus was full of happy people who had no idea where they were going.

After a whole day, they reached the sea.
"End of the road," said the driver, sadly.

"We can't stop now," said the lady with the pram.
"Let's take the ferry."

So they did.

"Where are you going?" asked a group of sailors on the ferry.

"Anywhere!" said the driver. "We're on an adventure!"

"Will you give us a lift?" asked the sailors.

"We'd love to," said the driver, "but we're full up."

So the sailors had a long think.

The sailors worked hard all night,
hammering, clanking and drilling.

And the next morning, it was
a gleaming triple-decker bus
that drove onto the shore.

Word got around that a
big bus was in town . . .

. . . and soon it was full again!
So the passengers got together
to build deck number four.

Things were going very happily on the four-decker bus, until . . .

"No problem," said the school children. "We've got an idea!" And they invented a clever way of going under (and over!) bridges.

"There's no stopping us now!" they said,
and decks five, six and seven soon followed.

After two months, the bus passed
through a very hot country. So deck
number thirty became a swimming
pool, with a deep end!

Six months later, the bus was taller than the tallest skyscraper.

And a
year after
they had set off, the
bus was 100 decks high.
The passengers had a huge
party that lasted all
night long.

It was the very next day
that the noise started.

CLUNK!
CLUNK!

"Oh dear,"
said the driver.

The day after that,
smoke started coming
from the engine.

"Dear, oh dear,"
said the driver.

And the day after that,
the bonnet blew off.

"Dear, oh dear, oh
dear," said the driver.

The poor bus had broken down!

Everyone got off and looked at each other.
"Where are we going?" they asked the driver.
"Nowhere," he replied, sadly.

Suddenly someone with
very sharp hearing said:

"Would you like a lift?"
shouted the man in
the balloon.

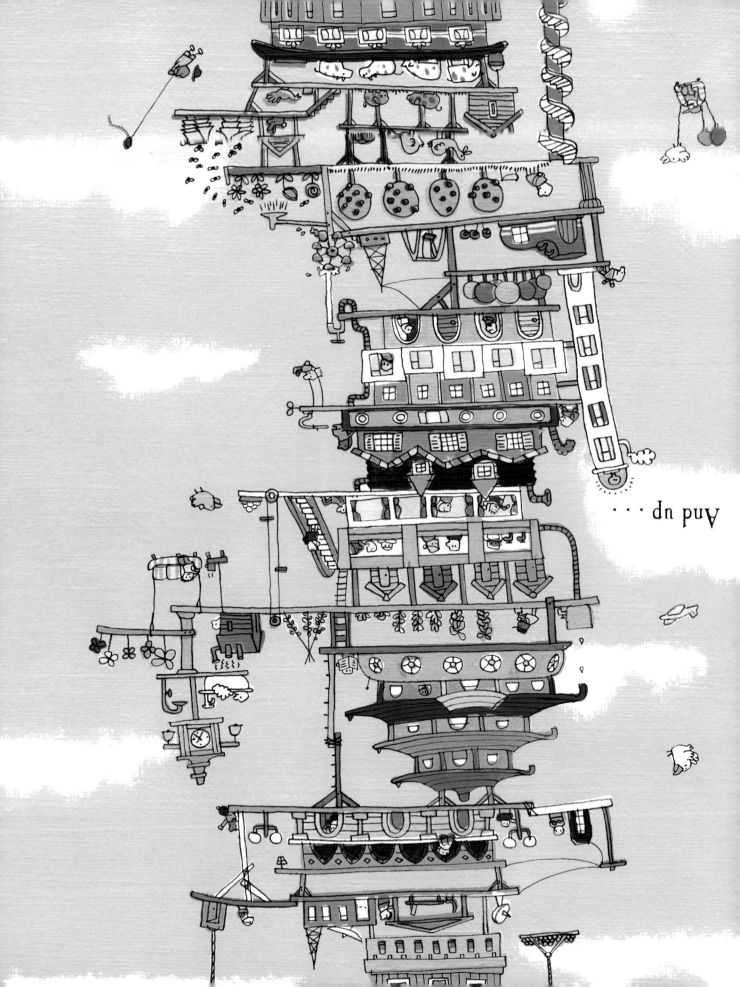

And up . . .

And up . . .

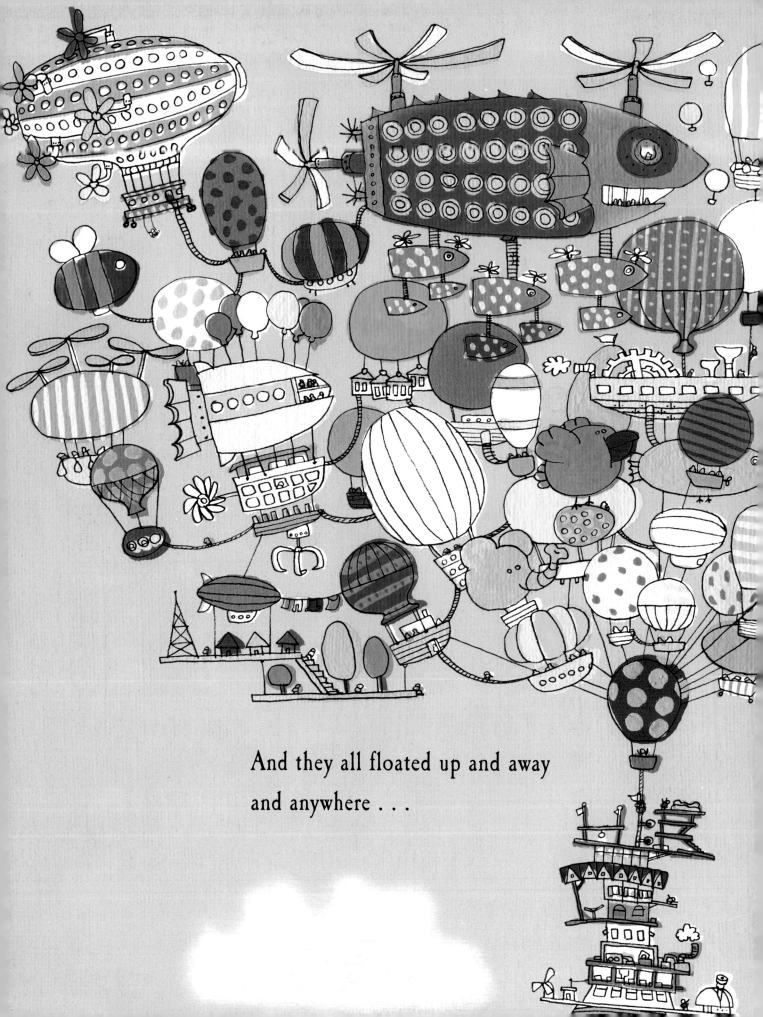

And they all floated up and away
and anywhere . . .

. . . because this was an adventure.